THOR

AN ORIGIN STORY

PaRragon

Bath • New York • Cologne • Melbourne • Delhi
Hong Kong • Shenzhen • Singapore

This is a story about someone who was born into royalty but needed to earn his honour. This is a story about a hero named **THOR.**

Thor's realm was called Asgard. It was like an island – its shores were swept by the sea of space.

The people who lived on Asgard were called Asgardians and the Asgardians called our world Midgard. The only way to reach our world from theirs was by the rainbow bridge, Bifrost.

The bridge was guarded by a sentry called Heimdall. Even though Asgard was well-protected, threats were endless. Thor was one of the land's great protectors.

He was also a prince. He lived with his brother, Loki, in the castle of their father, Odin.

Thor was arrogant and chose his friends for their loyalty: the brave warrior Balder and a band of soldiers called the Warriors Three – Fandral, Volstagg and Hogun – and the beautiful, strong and wise Lady Sif.

Thor's father, Odin, ruled over all of Asgard.
　　He and his wife, Frigga, wanted nothing more than for their sons
to grow up as worthy rulers.

But there could only be one supreme ruler of Asgard. Only one who could be like Odin. And even though Loki was thoughtful, clever and quick, Thor was firstborn and so the throne was his by right.

To decide when Thor would be ready to rule, Odin had a special hammer made. It was forged from a mystical metal called Uru, which came from the heart of a dying star.

The hammer was named Mjolnir and it held great power.

But no one would be able to lift the hammer unless he or she was worthy enough.

The hammer was immovable to Thor.

Still, Odin's actions made it clear: the hammer was meant for his firstborn son and no one else. This made Loki unhappy.

Even so, proving worthy of Mjolnir was not an easy task. Thor spent nearly every moment trying to earn his right to hold the hammer. He performed amazing acts of bravery ...

... he was honoured for acts of nobility and he demonstrated feats of great strength and honour.

With every great achievement, Thor attempted once more to pick up Mjolnir. It seemed as if he would never raise the hammer more than a few inches from the ground. And then one day ... he did.

Thor had proved himself worthy of his weapon and he used it well. When he threw the hammer, it always returned to him.

When he twirled it by its handle, he could soar like a winged beast! And when he stamped it twice upon the ground ...

... he could summon all the powers of LIGHTNING, RAIN AND THUNDER!

In fact, with his hammer in hand, there was little Thor could not do.

And he knew it. Odin wanted him to be a great warrior and he had become one. His father wanted him to earn the respect of Asgard.

He had it. But then Thor began to let the power go to his head. And Odin was not happy. In fact, he had grown quite angry with his son.

Odin called Thor to his throne room. Thor knew that something was wrong. His father rarely summoned him in such a harsh tone. Thor was sure that his jealous brother, Loki, had spun some lie to get him into trouble.

But nothing could have been further from the truth.

Odin told Thor that he was his favoured son. He told him that he was brave beyond compare and as noble as a prince must be.

He told him that his strength was legendary and that he was the best warrior in the kingdom. But Thor did not know what it meant to be weak or to feel pain. And without knowing humility, Thor could never be a truly honourable warrior.

Odin was angry. In his rage, he tore Mjolnir from Thor's hand and threw it towards Midgard. Then he stripped Thor of his armour and sent him to Earth.

Odin made his son believe that he was a medical student, with an injured leg, named Don Blake.

As Blake, Thor learned to study hard.

At times he thought he might fail. But he worked harder than he ever had in Asgard and, in the end, he earned his degree.

He allowed others to help him with his injury. In doing so, he discovered that people were generally good, and he learned to truly love humanity.

As a surgeon, Don treated the sick. He helped weak people find their strengths. Then one day, while on holiday in Norway ...

... Don Blake found himself trapped in a cave. The only possible exit lay behind a boulder.

Don found a staff on the ground and shoved it under the boulder. He tried with all his might to move the rock. He pushed and pushed.

Nothing. He was so angry that he took the staff and struck it on the ground. And that's when it became clear that it was no ordinary stick.

It was Mjolnir in disguise! Odin had sent Don to this cave on purpose. Odin, the All Father of Asgard, was pleased.

His son had learned humility. He had, at long last, become a complete hero. Now he was human in spirit, he would remain for evermore as …

... THE MIGHTY THOR